FLASH THE DASH

FLASH THE DASH

STORY AND PICTURES

By DON FREEMAN

A GOLDEN GATE JUNIOR BOOK

 Childrens Press, Chicago

Library of Congress Cataloging in Publication Data

Freeman, Don.
   Flash the Dash.

   SUMMARY: To his mate's surprise, Flash the
dachshund finally finds a steady job.
   "A Golden Gate junior book."
   (1. Dogs—Stories)   I. Title.
PZ7.F8747Fl   (E)   72-94227
ISBN 0-516-08722-3

To
Annie, Andrea and Ari

In the small town of Rocksun there once lived two dachshunds.

Although they looked somewhat alike, Flash and Sashay were not alike in many ways.

They lived together in a neat, low-slung bungalow in the back yard of an empty house at sixteen sixty Bixby Street.

Flash was the lazy one. Instead of going out each day to earn their daily bone, he took long naps.

Sashay ran errands all around the town, delivering newspapers and flowers. In return she was always given a bone or a liverwurst sandwich to take home.

One morning Sashay decided the time had come for Flash to do his share. "Today it's your turn to go out there and help earn our living," she said sternly.

Flash had been dreading this moment but he rose to his feet and went down the street to look for steady employment.

Block after block he searched for work. But even though everyone in town knew Flash, no one seemed to have any work for him to do.

Just as he was about to give up, he saw a sign in the window of the
Telegraph Office.

In he waddled, full of confidence and charm.

He took down the sign and held it in his mouth.

"Well, well! I'll be bamboozled!" said Mister Orkin, the telegraph operator. "It's Flash asking for work. Fancy that! I've got a good mind to take a chance on you."

After giving Flash a messenger's cap to wear, Mister Orkin said, "There! You're hired! Here's an important telegram that just came in over the wire. It's for the Mayor. Now, let's see you get a wiggle on!"

Flash waggled his tail and out the door he rushed.

Since he knew everyone in Rocksun and everyone knew him, Flash hardly needed to ask for directions.

Up the steep steps of the City Hall he leapt—not an easy thing for such a young underslung dachshund!

Down the corridor he ran and into the Mayor's office he raced. He
delivered the telegram to the Mayor's busy secretary.

Then out the door he tore and headed back to the Telegraph Office.

"Peapods and pickles!" exclaimed Mister Orkin. "That was fast! From now on I'm going to call you Flash the Dash!"

So, all that fall and on into winter Flash the Dash delivered telegrams to people in every part of Rocksun.

As for pay, Mister Orkin gave him pretzels and sausages to take home to Sashay.

Sashay was amazed and surprised to see Flash dash out the door each morning as soon as the sun came up.

Some mornings he arrived at the Telegraph Office ahead of Mister Orkin. And when this happened Flash would do a few limbering-up exercises. Of course push-ups were easy for him to do because he didn't have far to push up.

These exercises kept him in good shape. He needed to keep fit, especially when it came to trudging through the winter snow.

Through blinding blizzards and hailstorms Flash never failed to perform his duties.

Day after day and night after night he delivered his messages. There were nights when he was so tired he would crawl into an old crate to sleep, even though he was far from home.

Sashay never worried. She knew her mate would come home sooner or later.

But when spring came to the town of Rocksun, Flash began to get lazy again. Maybe he had a touch of spring fever.

One day he spent the whole morning lying in a field of daisies, watching the clouds roll by in the sky. No one, not even Sashay or Mister Orkin, knew where he was.

That same afternoon when he finally arrived at the Telegraph Office, he found a telegram placed under the door.

Without looking to see to whom the telegram was addressed,
Flash decided he needed a short rest before delivering it.
So he sauntered over to the park.

He just couldn't see why anyone needed a telegram on such a lovely day. *Nothing* could possibly be all *that* important!
He leaned against a tree and took a nap.

While he snoozed, a sudden breeze swept through the trees and blew the telegram away.

Luckily, a friendly lady caught the telegram inside her parasol just before it fell into the lily pond!

One look at the name and address and the lady knew who it was for . . .

"Flash! Flash!" she called. "Wake up! This telegram is for *you*!"

Flash sprang to his feet, stood on his hind legs and begged. The friendly lady understood what he meant. Opening the envelope, she began to read the message aloud. . .

Without so much as a thank-you bark, Flash flew across the park.

Straight to the hospital he sped.

There, inside the maternity ward, he beheld the happiest sight of his life—three one-day-old puppies snuggled up to their mother.

Needless to say, Sashay was very pleased to see their father. "You've been so busy lately, how did you ever know we were here, my dear?" she asked, all starry-eyed.

"Oh, I got the message!" replied Flash, blushing with pride. "I got the message!"

DON FREEMAN's way with a story, both in words and pictures, continues to delight scores of young readers and has earned him a permanent place in the hearts of children everywhere. He has written and illustrated more than thirty books, beginning with *Chuggy And The Blue Caboose* (with his wife Lydia), published by the Viking Press. He says that his story ideas come from his own many and varied experiences. For example, *Pet Of The Met* grew out of his visits backstage at the Metropolitan Opera House where he was assigned by the *New York Times* to draw his impressions of various Met productions. Mr. Freeman claims that his own inclination toward laziness, precisely at the wrong moments, inspired the story of *Flash The Dash*. Other Don Freeman titles published by Golden Gate are *Forever Laughter, Quiet! There's A Canary In The Library* and *Add-A-Line Alphabet*.